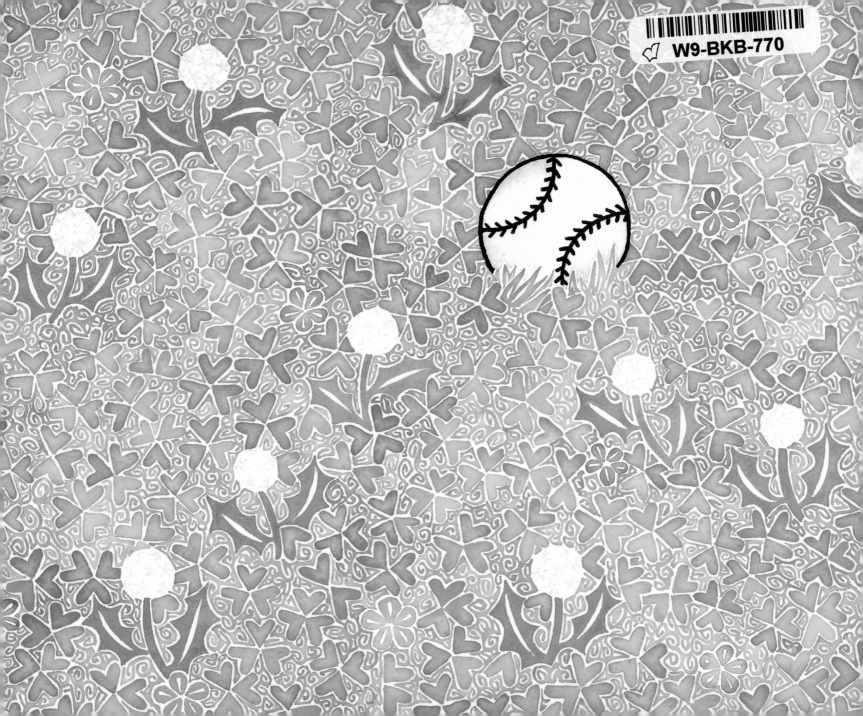

For my dad

My dad, Louis Mammano, 1944,
pitching for Lincoln High School,
Brooklyn, New York

Book design by Jessica Dacher.
Typeset in Gill Sans and ITC Officina.
The illustrations in this book were rendered in watercolor.
Manufactured in Hong Kong.

Library of Congress Cataloging-in-Publication Data
Mammano, Julie.
Rhinos who play baseball / by Julie Mammano.
p. cm.
Summary: Baseball-playing rhinos crack dingers out
of the park, rip grass-cutting grounders across the field,
and rally in the bottom of the ninth. Includes a glossary
of "catch phrases."
ISBN 0-8118-3605-3
[1. Baseball—Fiction. 2. Rhinoceroses—Fiction.] I. Title.
PZ7.M3117 Rb 2003
[E]—dc21
2002006886

Distributed in Canada by Raincoast Books
9050 Shaughnessy Street, Vancouver, British Columbia V6P 6E5

10 9 8 7 6 5 4 3 2 1

Chronicle Books LLC
85 Second Street, San Francisco, California 94105

www.chroniclekids.com

Rhinos Who Play Baseball

JULIE MAMMANO

chronicle books · san francisco

Rhinos who play baseball
dream of playing in the BIG LEAGUES.

They practice SLIDES and KNUCKLEBALLS.

They RIP GRASS-CUTTING GROUNDERS across the DIAMOND.

GO BIG GRAY!

RHINOS RULE!

SMACK!

and THROW HEAT from the HILL. They never get NOODLE ARM when they blast a YAKKER to the PLATE.

bangs out a **LINE DRIVE** straight up the **ALLEY.**

But for rhinos who play baseball, it's an **EASY OUT.**

They catch POP FLIES and nab SACRIFICE BUNTS.

Got it!

They set their WHEELS in motion to reach for a SHOESTRING CATCH.

When the rhinos get their UPS, the rowdy razzing from the INFIELD begins.

WAY TO GO!

Rhinos who play baseball crack
DINGERS OUT OF THE PARK.

When the rhinos STEAL A BASE,
they get caught in a PICKLE.
SAFE! That was a close call.

Now the rivals are ahead.

Rhinos who play baseball don't WIMP OUT, they put on their RALLY CAPS.

At the BOTTOM OF THE NINTH, their CLEANUP HITTER wins the game with a MOON SHOT. Going, going, gone!

Catch Phrases

big leagues major-league baseball teams

slide to reach the base by sliding into it

knuckleball a slow pitch using the knuckles

rip to hit hard

grass-cutting grounder a fast ground ball

diamond the playing field

season opener the first game of the season

take the field to run out to the field for a game

mound the pitcher's area in the center of the diamond

in the zone playing really well

windup when a pitcher swings back his arm and lifts his foot for a pitch

throw heat to pitch a good fastball

hill the pitcher's mound

noodle arm when a pitcher's arm gets tired

yakker a curve ball

plate where a batter stands when hitting and a runner must touch to score

rookie slugger-wannabe a new player acting like a big hitter

line drive a ball hit sharply so it flies low and fast and in a straight line

alley the area between the outfielders

easy out a play in which a batter or base runner is easily tagged out

pop fly a short, high fly ball

sacrifice bunt to tap the ball to the infield to advance the runner

wheels legs

shoestring catch a running catch made near the ground

up turn at bat

infield the area of the field inside the diamond

eyes on the ball watching the ball

choke to mess up

dinger a home run

out of the park past the outfield

steal a base to advance to the next base as the pitcher throws the ball to the batter

pickle when a runner gets caught between bases by the fielders

safe when a runner doesn't get tagged out

seventh-inning stretch when the spectators stretch and often sing in the middle of the seventh inning

bases loaded when first, second and third bases all have runners

grand slam a home run when the bases are loaded

strike out when the batter misses all the pitches and doesn't get to first base

slump to play really badly for a long time

wimp out to quit too easily

rally cap to wear a baseball cap in a silly way to show support for a losing team

bottom of the ninth the second half of the last inning of a game

cleanup hitter a player who's known for hitting home runs

moon shot a very long, high home run

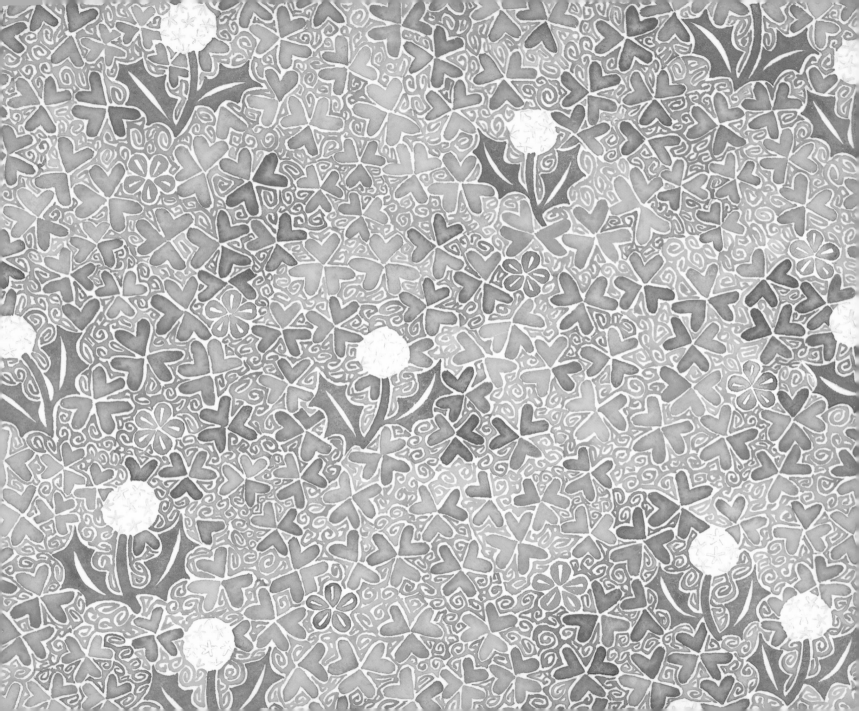